To Mary Jane and
Highlights Foundation
—E.M.

Copyright © 2019 Erin McGill
Book design by Melissa Nelson Greenberg

Photograph of the Lanvin dress
on page 22: © Chicago Historical Society,
all rights reserved

Library of Congress Cataloging-in-Publication Data available.

ISBN: 978-1-944903-72-5

Printed in China

10 9 8 7 6 5 4 3 2 1

Cameron Kids is an imprint of Cameron + Company

Cameron + Company
Petaluma, CA 94952
www.cameronbooks.com

Matchy Matchy

Erin McGill

cameron kids

My name is Maria, but you might as well call me Matchy Matchy.

At school, I match.

Laces and lunchbox.
Backpack and barrettes.

At playtime, I match.

Every holiday, I match.

Even my underwear matches.

My mom picks out all of my clothes.

She makes everyone . . . and everything match.

But I do not want to be so matchy matchy.

I want to mix it up!

None of my friends have to match.

No matching socks. No matching patterns. No matching anything!

But me . . .
I'm about to lose my matchy-matchy mind.

I rebel. I conceal.

I debate. I march.

Mom matches my efforts.

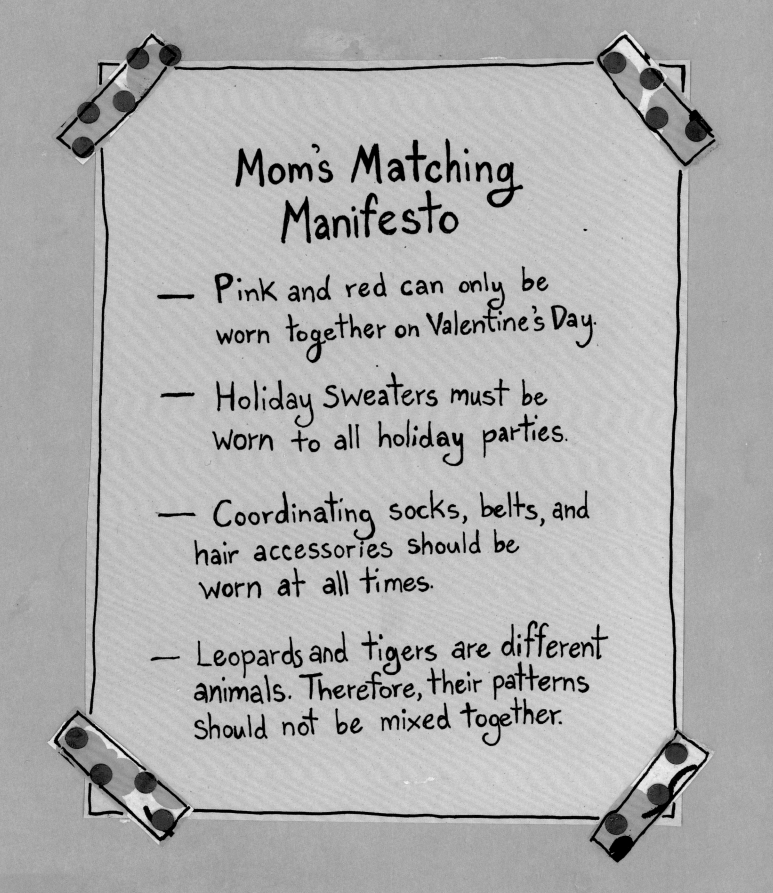

I must make Mom see . . .

what not being matchy matchy means to me.

Maria's
Spring collection
debut!
Fashion Show
Today
2 pm

Feathers and fringe!

Pom-poms and plaid!

Spikes and spots!

Tiaras and tails!

Leopard and lace!

"Polka dots
and petunias!"

Mom?

Amazing.

My name is Maria,
and this is me.
Marvelous, unmatching, mix-it-up me!